Praise for ICE and J

"Thriller and a chiller. One you will not put down until you finish reading the book." - Blaine Jones, M.D.

"A new tactful thriller." - Amazon.com

"A fifteen year old boy has this fantastic ability to write a book that reads of a much older person."- Amazon.com

"Jack Drummond is a powerful up-and-coming literary talent in Appalachia." - F. Keith Davis, author of The Secret Life and Brutal Death of Mamie Thurman

"Jack Drummond is an amazing talent. Reading ICE and interviewing him on the radio you forget how young he is! I look forward to future books from Jack's creative mind." - Brian Sumner WCQR Program Director/Johnson City TN

"I've seen the future of speculative fiction, and his name is Jack Drummond." – Bram Stoker Award-winning author and editor, Michael Knost

"Jack has a lot of talent and his future is bright. He will definitely make his mark in the writing world." – Kyle Lovern, author and journalist

JACK DRUMMOND

SHADOWS

JACK DRUMMOND

SHADOWS

Jack Drummond

JACK DRUMMOND

SHADOWS

JACK DRUMMOND

ACKNOWLEDGMENTS

I would like to take this opportunity to thank and recognize all who had a hand in making this book come together.

First and foremost, God. Without Him, I am nothing.

I would also like to thank Mom, Dad, Mike, Derica, and Madison; you guys are the best. I would also like to give a very big thanks to all my friends, namely Chace, Maclain, and Emily (one of my editors and closest friends). I find my inspiration in you every day. A special thanks to the Grables and the McKinneys, who kept me safe during the winter storm of the decade. One very big thank you to my teachers, you have the patience of Job when it comes to me. Thank all of guys with Powell Construction's Johnson City office; you're some of my biggest fans and some of my most avid encouragers. Let me give a special thanks to Burch Middle School of Delbarton, West Virginia. You guys are awesome. And also I want to give a very special thank you to the guys in Washington, D.C. for all your input and much-needed info. Keep it up Herb. Let me also give a thank you to Roy and Grounded Youth for encouraging me and keeping me straight on the path this whole time. A special shout out to Steven James and the Huhns, you have helped and encouraged more than you know. Brian and Mike at 88.3 WCQR out of Gray, Tennessee, you guys have given me so much inspiration and publicity and have my undying gratitude. The Open Book of Williamson, West Virginia has my undying gratitude as well.

And to all my other friends, family, and fans, I owe you all more than I can ever repay.

I hope you guys are ready for more.

Because as of right now, this series is just getting started...

SHADOWS

JACK DRUMMOND

PROLOGUE

300 miles off the coast of the United States, in the Atlantic Ocean. . .

The still waters reflected the moon and the stars above, the constellations and the heavens. Somewhere in the distance, a whale could be heard, sending her fain call across the waters. And then there was silence.

That stillness was suddenly broken.

A large, circular object the size of a football field rocketed from the sky above into the waters of the Atlantic. The impact sent water spraying high into the night sky, the flames on the hull of the strange metallic vessel illuminating the ocean in the darkness. Nearly a mile overhead, two F-16 fighter jets rocketed past the wreckage.

"Bogey is down!" the pilot of the first F-16 said into his headset.

"That was some good shootin', Rex!" the first pilot's wingman shouted into his own headset.

Amidst the wreckage, as the metallic hulk began to sink beneath the waves, a hatch on the vessel's hull opened, and a tall figure dressed in black emerged from the interior.

"Hold on, command," Rex said into his headset, "looks like we've got a live one down there."

"Typically search and destroy means to find and annihilate," a female's cool and collected voice said over each pilot's headset, "not to do a partial job."

"Sorry about that command," the wingman said with a slight chuckle.

"We're coming around," Rex said, pulling his F-16 into a sharp turn. "Missiles locked."

"Fire at will," the woman's voice said.

Rex thumbed a small red button on the controls, and two missiles rocketed from each wing of his craft. He watched as the flames spouting from the tail ends of both missiles grew smaller as the missiles themselves sped toward their target. The figure on the hull of the downed craft looked up to see the missiles rocketing toward him, and lifted a short metallic rod that he drew from his waistband.

He pointed the rod at the oncoming missiles and pressed a minute button near the bottom of the rod. He held the rod, and a moment later it bucked hard in his grip. A miniscule white ball of brilliant light burst from the tip of the rod, flying toward the oncoming missiles.

Rex watched on in awe. "Uh… command?"

The white ball began to contort, expand, and grow. An instant later it became a massive wall-like structure in the form of a square. The missiles slammed into the light, but were merely absorbed into it instead of exploding upon impact.

"Go ahead, Rex," the woman's voice said.

The wall of light then suddenly exploded into a brilliant array of white, sending the light in every direction.

Rex yanked up on the controls as the explosion of light engulfed his F-16.

"What the…?"

His F-16 suddenly exploded.

His wingman's craft hung a hard left but could not escape the light's reach.

The craft was bathed in the light, and burst into flames a moment later.

Then the light dissipated.

The figure was still standing on the hull of his downed craft. He simply replaced the rod in his waistband and watched as both fighter jets fell from the sky in burning heaps of flames.

TWO WEEKS LATER…

JACK DRUMMOND

ONE

He awoke with a start and bolted upright.

Malcolm Reed blinked twice, glanced around the tiny room that he found himself. There was nothing more than a bed, a TV in the corner, and a desk against the far wall. There was a bathroom in the adjoining room.

Sunlight was streaming in through the thin drapes over the only window in the room, giving the room a golden flare that did something to make its shabbiness seem not as bad as one would originally expect.

His head began to throb, and he tried to shake off the feeling. He swung his feet down to the floor, only then realizing that he was wearing shoes; loafers, to be precise. He cocked his head as he looked at his shoes, his mind spiraling into focus.

Then, suddenly…

"Chase…" he muttered.

It all came flooding back to him in a half-second.

Alaska.

The Atoka Research Facility.

The creature.

The man in black.

The light.

Chase.

He more or less exploded off of the rough bed, managing to take one small step before stumbling. He had to catch himself against the wall in order to keep from falling flat on his face. He took in several quick breaths and shook his head again before regaining his balance and starting forward. He approached the window next to the door and tore back the curtain, peering outside.

His immediate thought, was that it was just the immense heat present in the small space that was getting to him, making him delusional in the aspect that he saw nothing beyond a desert out the window, essentially an empty wasteland.

But he quickly realized that he was located in the middle of nowhere. He half expected to see a dust devil blow past or a ball of thickets reminiscent of an old Clint Eastwood western. There was nothing but the desert that lay before him, with the exception of the few bushes and brambles and cacti, as well as the ridged mountains of somewhere far off. He half shielded his eyes against the blazing sunlight as he squinted past the mirage. In the distance, he thought he saw what appeared to be an old stone church. There were a few trees on past the church, but besides that only blue sky.

Perspiration had matted his hair and gathered between his shoulder blades. He was tempted to shed the blue long-sleeved shirt he was wearing, but the stench in the room kept him from doing it. His paranoia led him to think that there were some infectious bacteria floating about from the stench alone. He rolled up the sleeves of his shirt and turned. He took a brief moment to walk around the room. He poked his head in the bathroom, but immediately drew back out and slammed the door, suddenly aware of where the awful smell was coming from.

He started back across the room, pausing only momentarily to switch on the television in the corner. There was only static on the screen. He tried to flip through a few of the channels using the switch next to the screen, but all that emitted from the television was static and fuzz. He muttered a curse to himself, slammed his palm against the television once, but ultimately switched it off when it became obvious that brute force was not what it took in order to reestablish a good antenna connection.

By then Reed was convinced that the air conditioning unit was broken, and that if he wanted to know where he was or how he got there or…anything else, really, then he would have to venture outside to…God-only-knew-where.

He proceeded across the room to the door, scouring the room for a phone of any sort along the way. When his quest for a phone came up empty, he stood in front of the door for a long moment, breathing heavily, his brain pounding against his skull. Then he reached forward and pulled the door open, the golden sunlight flooding him along with the immense heat of the barren desert that lay before him. He stood there for a long moment, basking in the rays of sunlight raining down from the cloudless blue skies.

Then, his eyes closed, he started forward.

TWO

Quantico, Virginia
FBI Academy

The long hours of lesson planning and the few hours of sleep that former FBI Special Agent Elizabeth Chase had received were beginning to take their toll on her. It was just midday, but as she drew her red pen across the last of her students' papers, she was looking forward to retiring early for a few hours before waking and returning to the academy to teach her final class of the day.

After finishing with the papers, she reshuffled them before placing them down neatly on the corner of her desk. With a sigh, she removed her reading glasses and rubbed gently her tired eyes. Replacing the glasses on the bridge of her nose, she pushed herself away from the desk and rose from the leather chair that had lost all means of offering comfort over two hours before. She switched off the lamp on the far corner of the desk and closed the screen of her laptop computer after initiating a lock on its files.

The sunlight streamed in through the

drapes pulled together over the large window on the wall to her left, casting a dazzling array of golden colors throughout the room that sparkled and reflected off of the numerous shiny objects she had placed all about her office space. Taking up her overcoat from the back of the chair that was situated on the opposite side of her desk, she shrugged the coat over her shoulders and removed the reading glasses from her face. From the inner pocket of her coat, she withdrew a small brown glasses case, slipped her glasses into it, and placed it back inside her coat.

Instinctively, she flipped her shoulder-length, auburn hair out from underneath the collar of her coat before finally turning and starting across the room toward the door. She reached out, taking hold of the handle, and then opened the door.

She immediately took two steps back in surprise.

A man stood on the other side, his fist lifted as if he were preparing to knock. The man on the other side appeared equally as startled, but did not move as he stood there watching her. There was a long, awkward silence between the two of them, during which the man lowered his hand to his side and straightened his tie.

"Can I help you?" Chase asked after breathing a sigh of relief.

"Are you Agent Chase?" the man responded inquisitively.

"Yes."

"Greg Knowles," the man said, extending his hand. "DOD."

Chase returned the gesture, taking note of how neat the man presented himself:

His dark hair was combed *neatly* to one side; he was clean-shaven, clean-cut in appearance and in his presenting manner. The dark business suit he wore was perfectly tailored, without so much as a misplaced stitch visible on the seams. Chase doubted that she could find a stitch of clothing misplaced on the suit even if she had a microscope with her and was performing a close evaluation. The suit wrapped neatly around his slender form, his tie perfectly straightened.

Chase almost laughed out loud.

She'd seen them all before, and the man before her, like so many others in Washington, was the embodiment of the government's best.

"Well, Mr. Knowles," she said, retrieving the hand that had been in his grip for far too long in her opinion, "what could I do for the Depart of Defense?"

"May I come in, please?"

Chase studied his face for a long moment. Ever since she had awakened in the bedroom of her townhouse six months before, she had been dealing with men like this almost every week. Things had just gotten to where the government was starting to leave her alone. She did not really feel like having to deal with the man, as she was looking forward to getting home and resting.

"Look," she began, "I've answered all of the questions that I'm going to answer and I thought I'd made that explicitly clear to the government."

"I understand that, Agent Chase," Knowles said, nodding quickly, "but I'm here on a more pressing matter."

Chase studied him hard. He seemed sincere enough. But she *really* did not want to get caught up for an hour or two answering questions that she had already answered a dozen times over. She was determined not to get held up by the man.

"I'm sorry, Mr. Knowles, but I really

must be going…"

"Agent Chase," the man broke in, his words more forceful this time, "it will only take a moment."

At that instant there was a gleam in the man's Eye that told Chase his stubbornness greatly exceeded his clean-cut and formal exterior appearance. There was no way that he was going to leave until she answered his question. Reluctantly, Chase stepped aside and gestured slightly for Knowles to enter.

"Thank you," he uttered as he stepped past her.

Rolling her eyes, she closed the door behind him before turning and following him back into her office. As he sat down in the chair across from her desk, she switched on the lamp situated on the corner of her desk before taking off her overcoat and strolling over to her leather chair. She sat down in the chair and laid her overcoat across her lap.

"Now," she said, interlocking her fingers and placing her forearms down on the surface of the desk. She watched Knowles produced a manila folder from the inside of his long overcoat and asked, "What is this about?"

THREE

Reed glanced left, then right down the boardwalk on which he found himself. He suddenly realized that he had not been in a little house all to himself, but had been in what appeared to be a single room amongst many others at a small hotel. There were only about a dozen rooms in total, and the old wooden support beams running along the boardwalk held the unstable-looking roof over his head. At the far left end of the boardwalk, there appeared to be another building, one that looked just as old as the church through the mirage. Reed stared hard for a long moment at the building, which appeared to be made of stone.

He then looked back across the way, peering through the mirage at the old church in the distance. Turning, he started down the boardwalk in the direction of the building. The roof ahead was unstable in appearance, so much so that Reed was tempted to step off the boardwalk and continue on from there.

The boards underneath him creaked as he went along, moaning every time he placed his foot down.

It suddenly occurred to him that he could very easily fall through.

Suddenly he stopped. For a long moment he stood there on the boardwalk. Golden sunlight streamed in through the cracks in the rickety roof over his head. A gentle breeze blew through his dark hair, cooling his face.

The heat caused his head to throb all the more.

Somewhere in the distance, an eagle screeched.

He swore softly to himself.

Why was he so paranoid?

He knew himself to be a cautious individual, but not to the extent that he was worrying about falling through an old and rickety boardwalk.

He could remember the past and evaluate the present. He could even speculate the future. Yet it was as though something were missing, as though a part of him was just... *gone.*

He started forward again, this time emerging at the other end of the boardwalk to find a quaint little town. The town's being right there so suddenly threw him for a loop, but at least its presence explained why there were a hotel and an old church nearby. But how on earth did he get here?

Why was he here?

His last memory was of being in Alaska, in a room in the Atoka Research Facility.

Now he found himself in a barren desert, utterly in the middle of nowhere.

The town only raised more questions.

It looked deserted, as there were no pedestrians crowding the streets, only a bunch of desolate, ancient-looking buildings of stone. There were, however, a few modern-looking buildings, with some older models of vehicles ranging from Ford trucks to Land Rovers to even an older model Grand Prix.

There came a sound behind him, a sound of rubber meeting wood.

Reed wheeled around, his hand dropping reflexively for his gun, only to palm noThing but air. Instead of a hostile force, he was encountered only by a soccer ball bounding toward him. Bouncing once more, the ball shot airborne and Reed extended both arms instinctively. He caught the ball in mid-fall.

He glanced around for the owner of

the grimy, stained soccer ball, but no one fell into his line of sight.

"Hey," a voice came from behind him.

Reed turned slowly to see a small boy, no more than ten or eleven years old, staring hard at him. He held the child's gaze for a long moment, through the throbbing and the aching finally making the connection that the soccer belonged to the boy only when the boy's eyes fell upon the ball.

Reed actually felt compassion and sympathy for the child when he noticed the look of longing for the ball in the child's eyes. He took one step toward the boy, who took one step back. Reed tried again, two steps further, only for the boy to match him step for step in backward motion. He finally stopped when he caught the glimpse of curiosity and uncertainty cross the boy's round face. It was as though the boy was unsure of Reed's intentions, unsure of whether or not to ask for the ball back, unsure of what Reed's response would be should he decide to ask for the ball in return.

"It's okay," Reed said, extending the ball toward the boy. "Here."

The boy studied Reed's face for a

long moment, squinting past the optical illusion commonly found in moisturized sand portions of the desert. After a moment, it became apparent to Reed that the boy was not going to approach him. So, he dropped the soccer ball to his feet and gave it a gentle kick that sent it rolling in the boy's direction. Even as the ball rolled toward the boy, the child's eyes never left Reed's own.

At the last second, the ball rolled over a rock that sent it spiraling to the left. Before the ball rolled past the boy, he extended his foot and stopped it, yet he still held Reed in his uncertain gaze.

"Look," Reed started again, "I'm an FBI agent, and I seem to be…" he looked around him, hoping for some geographical landmark or to be blessed with some knowledge that would offer him a sign as to where he was, "a little lost."

The boy offered no response.

"Can you help me?"

Nothing.

Zip.

Zilch.

"Here," Reed said as he started forward.

The moment he took one step

forward, the boy scooped up the ball in one smooth motion before turning quickly and sprinting off in the opposite direction. He dashed around the side of a stone building and out of sight, the red shirt that was nearly two sizes too big for his small form billowing behind him.

Reed took a few more steps forward, wanting to pursue the boy. Why had he run? What had been so intimidating about Reed?

Muttering a curse, Reed drove his foot, toe-first, into the scorched sands on which he stood, kicking dirt up and creating a dust cloud so dense that he had to immediately turn to avoid absorbing the dirt and grit with his eyes.

So childish of him.

He did not care. He just wanted to know where he was, why he could not remember...

What he could not remember...

FOUR

Quantico, Virginia
FBI Academy

Knowles passed the manila folder across the desk to Chase, who flipped it open and skimmed across the numerous pages contained within. There were numerous snapshots of the Atoka Research Facility, some in black and white, others in full color, both before and after the military had burned it due to what had been officially classified as a *biological hazard*. After the pictures of the Atoka Research Facility came the shots of the bodies of numerous individuals that she recognized.

Marie and Derek Hardy… they had tried to kill her and her partner Malcolm Reed.

Janice Shaft… it was anyone's guess as to what had happened to her; a comatose-like state; possibly murdered by the Hardys.

Guy Hamilton… the ranger whom Reed had ultimately shot and killed after a frantic standoff and foot chase.

There were a couple of shots of a badly burned and disfigured body that Chase could only guess was Jim Hodgson... the pilot who had flown the team to the facility and had been killed when their helicopter was downed. Reed had theorized the crash as being the result of a plastic explosive.

And then, there was Alan Donovan... the man Chase had fallen so hard for. The man who played them all right up until the very end. The man who had initiated the ultimate betrayal toward her and her partner. The man who had been shot and killed by someone who seemed then to be as much of a ghost as Malcolm Reed himself.

On the final page, encompassing almost the entiRe upper half of the page, was a picture of her partner who had been missing for six months. Malcolm Reed had short dark hair cropped close to his cranium in this particular picture. It was the same picture that Chase had seen dozens of times on her partner's FBI ID badge.

His dark eyes stared blankly up at her from the page, lingering on her, so full of the knowledge of the hardships that came with everyday life.

His strong face was expressionless.

Chase bit her bottom lip upon seeing the picture, her eyes lingering on Reed's face for what seemed like an eternity. Across the bottom of the page, in bold, black ink was the word **MISSING**. She forced herself to close the folder.

She looked up at Knowles, whom she found was watching her intently.

Sliding the folder back across the surface of the desk, she rocked backward in her chair.

"Why are you here, Mr. Knowles?" she asked, suddenly irritated at herself for letting the man into her office space.

"I was reading the report you filed upon your... *return*," said Knowles, speaking the final word as if he had thought hard on just which word to use. "Can you tell me just how you managed to get back to D.C.?"

"I've already answered this," Chase replied stubbornly. "I've told you people, I don't remember."

"Are you sure?"

Chase bit back a curse.

"Yes," she said, speaking very slowly and leaning forward a little, "I'm sure."

"Absolutely?"

Chase took a slow, long, deep breath.

"Mr. Knowles," she began, "I

wouldn't have allowed you to come in had I known that you were going to interrogate me."

Knowles stared hard at her for a long moment, his cold blue eyes seeming to twinkle with a hint of malice.

"Of course Agent Chase. I apologize. I didn't mean for this to go in that direction. But, I *do* need help clearing up this one little discrepancy..."

"Go ahead," Chase said after a moment's silence on Knowles's part.

"You mentioned a... *creature*... of some sort in your official report. Could you go into a bit more detail on the subject of this creature?"

Chase took a brief moment to collect her thoughts, to try and remember all that she could about what had occurred back at the Atoka Research Facility in Alaska. Then, a moment later, she launched into her explanation.

FIVE

The building nearest him had a sign that read *Sandra's Diner* in the window. With the back of his hand, Reed wiped a drizzle of sweat from his forehead and then started for the diner, glancing both ways down the street. Extending his hand, he pushed gently open the door to the diner. A bell rigged to go off whenever the door was opened rang quietly from somewhere in the back of the diner to announce his entry.

To his surprise, he was met with several blank stares.

Stares.

From at least a half-dozen patrons occupying the majority of what few booths were situated inside of the diner. He did not know whether to throw up his hand or just turn around and walk right back out. The stares he received were cold ones, malicious in every aspect of the word.

It was only when the smell of freshly-made bacon reached his nostrils did Reed realized just how hungry he was. Inhaling deeply, he welcomed the warm aroma of the salty strips of hog meat. That was when he made up his mind that the only time he was going to leave that little diner was after he had eaten his share and filled his growling stomach.

How long had it been since he had eaten?

He did not know.

All he knew was that he was starving, and his sudden want for food outweighed his want to know how he came to be where he was. Perhaps, the thought crossed his mind, he did not want to remember.

Maybe that was why he could not remember in the first place.

To him, it made logical sense. He could not remember, because he did not want to remember.

Yes.

That *must* be it.

But still, that explanation begged the question: why did he not want to remember?

What could possibly have happened that he just did not want to remember?

Did it concern his partner?

The creature?

The man in black?

At that instant, a short, plump woman as rotund as she was tall came waddling through the archway leading from the dining area to the kitchen, carrying with her two trays, containing two plates each. Those plates held an assortment of breakfast foods ranging from gravy and biscuits to sausage and eggs, as well as strips of bacon along with an assortment of different butters and jams. The very sight of the smorgasbord of breakfast foods made Reed want to eat all the more.

The passing waitress glanced in his direction, but seemed not to care as she went about her way delivering the food to the patrons of the diner. Reed could still feel the eyes of many of the diner patrons upon him as he stood in the entryway to the diner. Suddenly he became fully aware at just how injudicious he must have looked, standing there, unmoving, eyeing the food as it was brought past him. In an attempt to make himself appear intelligent in some way, he walked over to the bar that was void of any person whatsoever and sat down on a stool.

He glanced around at the diner's patrons, the majority of whom were still watching him with an uncertain look in their eyes, a look of curiosity intertwined with caution, not unlike the look in the eyes of the small boy Reed had crossed paths with outside the diner just prior to entering. Turning away, Reed folded his arms and placed them on the surface of the bar before him. After delivering the orders to their respective diner patrons, the plump little waitress waddled her way over behind the bar and stacked the now empty trays on top of one another before sliding them down the bar against the other stacks of identical trays. Finally, she turned around to face Reed and wiped her hands on the apron she wore.

"Can I get you anything, hun?" she asked, placing her hands on her hips.

Reed was in want of food more than anything.

He was starving.

But he had already gone through his pockets, and knew that he was penniless.

"I…" he started, "I… well… um…"

"It's on the house, honey," the woman said with a crooked grin.

On the house…

Well, in that case…

"Could I get a couple biscuits with gravy and…" Reed contemplated his next choice, reveling in the opportunity, "…maybe a couple pieces of bacon?"

The woman nodded quickly, eying Reed for a long moment with calculating green eyes behind a pair of round spectacles that enlarged her eyes to what Reed could only estimate was twice their normal size.

"You sure that's all I can get you?" she asked after a hesitation.

Reed thought hard. What really sounded good right then?

"Go ahead and add two eggs with that," he added after a moment.

"How do you want them?"

"Over easy."

The woman nodded slowly, then turned and started back through the archway to the kitchen.

"Wait," he called after her.

She turned and looked at him.

"What day is it?"

"The twenty-first."

"Of September?"

She inclined her head while she looked at him. "It's February, honey. Where've you been?"

"The year?"

She nodded toward a calendar posted on the far wall and disappeared into the kitchen. Reed glanced over at the year and then sat back in his seat in disbelief.

He had missed Christmas.

He had missed the New Year.

He rested his head in his hands.

He strained his mind to remember, tried to break down the barriers to portions of his memory that he was so sUre did not exist.

Yet he could not.

No matter how hard he tried, he could not remember.

Six months.

Gone.

Missing.

Six months of his life were missing.

SIX

Quantico, Virginia
FBI Academy

Knowles rocked backward in his chair, settling down a little and seemingly becoming a bit more comfortable. Chase ran a hand over her face, glad that the drawn out explanation she had given was finally over. Now she wanted nothing more than to just get out of there.

"Let me get this straight," Knowles said after a moment. "This creature *possessed* a man, exploded out of his stomach, somehow managed to evade capture by *three* FBI agents, was captured by Agent Donovan, but was taken by an unknown man after he killed Agent Donovan because Agent Donovan was going to kill Agent Reed and yourself?"

Chase nodded slowly.

"And what did you say this... man told you again?"

"That the government had betrayed us, and that we were not safe."

"And that's when he gave you this keycard of sorts that took you to a room that was not on record, and that's how you were transported... where?"

"I told you. I don't know."

"And this occurred...when? The twenty-sixth of August?"

"The twenty-seventh."

"Six months ago next Tuesday?"

"Right."

Knowles nodded slowly to himself.

"Can I ask about the man who took the creature?" he said.

Chase sighed, irritated.

"Look," she said, bringing a hand up to her forehead, "I really need to be getting home. Could we just continue this another time?"

Knowles stared hard at her, his chin resting on his interlocked fingers, his elbows resting on the arms of the chair he was sitting in.

"I would rather get this finished and over with now," he said quietly.

Chase was growing all the more irritated, and was fighting to suppress her growing fury.

"I'm sorry," she said, "but I've answered all I'm going to answer. I'm leaving now."

She rose from her seat and tugged on her overcoat. Knowles stood at almost exactly same time as she, stuffing into his overcoat the manila folder he had previously allowed Chase to view. Chase switched off the lamp and started around her desk, only to be stopped by Knowles when he stepped in front of her path. Chase eyed him for a long moment.

"I'm leaving, Mr. Knowles," she repeated. "I'll show you the door on the way out."

"I'm sorry, Agent Chase."

Chase glared at him.

"Mr. Knowles," she said, "you need to leave. Now."

Knowles did not respond, but instead held his ground, staring down at Chase over the bridge of his small nose. Chase's heart beat more rapidly now, the awkwardness of the situation becoming more and more dubious with every passing second. Her instincts told her to run, that she had placed herself in a vulnerable position.

In a blur of motion, Knowles had wrapped his right hand around Chase's throat. She struggled against his strong grip as he lifted her off the floor, her legs flailing.

She tried for his groin, striking home with her stilettos. The blow seemed not to affect him, as he continued to grip her even tighter. She gasped for air, Knowles's grip closing off the oxygen flow into her trachea. She tried to break his hold, to struggle out of his grip. But she began to lose consciousness, the very will to fight.

In an amazing feat of strength, Knowles hurled her across the room, slamming her into the opposite wall. Books toppled off the nearby shelf, and a vase of flowers jumped off a nearby tabletop, shattering into dozens of small pieces on the floor and splashing the little water contained in the vase over the floor and onto the walls. The impact jarred Chase beyond the state of being dazed, but not to the extent that she lost consciousness. Picking herself up off the floor, Chase looked up just in time to see Knowles approaching her, just feet away. The malicious look in his eye made Chase feel even more insecure.

She was cornered.

There was no way out.

The door lay on the other side of The room.

And Knowles stood between her and

SHADOWS

her only means of escape.

JACK DRUMMOND

SEVEN

It had not been but about ten minutes since he had ordered, when the plump little woman who had taken Reed's order came through the archway once more with his food on a plate. The sight of a warm meal had never looked so splendid to him. He could only guess as to how long it had been since he had last eaten, but from the way his insides felt, he estimated that it had been a long while.

The woman set the plate of food down in front of him on the bar, the aroma given off by the food filling his nostrils and offering him warmth that seemed like, only moments before, had been an eternity away.

"What can I get you to drink?" the woman asked as she placed a rolled up napkin containing the silverware next to his plate. "Coffee? Orange juice?"

"A coffee," Reed said, tempted to explode out of his chair and dance around in a circle.

Coffee!

How long had it been since he had had coffee?

He was not sure, but one thing was for

sure… it had been *too* long.

The woman nodded and started back through the archway.

"A creamer?" she asked over her shoulder.

"No," Reed called after her.

"You got it, sweetheart."

And with that, the woman disappeared back through the archway.

Unrolling the napkin, Reed took up his silverware and dug in. The eggs were just a fraction off, missing just a touch of pepper that he added from the pepper shaker that was sitting just to his right, next to the salt shaker. The gravy was superb, just like everything seemed to be with him as hungry as he was. The biscuits were a bit hard, but softened to a likable extent when coated with the gravy. He ate with pleasure, rejoicing with every bite he took.

Even as he sat eating with his back to the rest of the diner's patrons, he could feel their eyes burning into him.

He dared not turn around.

Three bites later, the woman reappeared in the archway carrying a coffee mug larger than any Reed had ever seen before. He was all too glad when she set it down next him and he took a small sip of the steaming black liquid.

Coffee, to him, was an addiction.

The minutes ticked by, with only the small talk made by the diner's patrons the only source of noise within the small and enclosed area. Although a song was coming in and out of static over the diner's old stereo system, it was more background noise than anything else, sufficiently heard but not to the extent that it obscured Reed's own thoughts.

He ate slowly, still wracking his brain for explanations.

Reasons.

Answers.

WHy was it so difficult for him to remember?

The chatter in the room did little to ease his throbbing head, making it all the more difficult to try and concentrate his thoughts. He took another bite, chewed slowly. Pondering…

Suddenly there was a nausea welling up within him, turning his stomach flip-flops. The feeling had come over him so suddenly, so unexpectedly, that he had had little time to react. He sprang off his stool, dropping his fork into the gravy and knocking his coffee over, spilling it all over the surface of the bar. He wheeled around, fighting the urge to vomit. He looked quickly around the diner for some sign indicating a nearby restroom, but saw none. By that point, he knew that his only chance was the front door. Starting forward, he half-ran, half-stumbled his way through the diner, trying desperately to reach the door.

His head spun, the world around him bouncing in and out of focus, the undercurrent of chatter had become only a mesh of loud, rumbling sounds. Even the song that had been almost inaudible just moments before now seemed to roar loudly, an ear-splitting gurgle of sound. He was just feet from the door now, stumbling forward, though now unsure that he could make it.

What was happening to him?

He tripped over the leg of a nearby booth and went reeling to floor, landing hard on the wooden boards. The fall dazed him slightly, but as determined as ever he pushed himself up off the floor and stumbled forward once more. He threw himself against the door, which swung open under his weight, spilling him out onto the boardwalk outside not a moment too soon, for as soon as he cleared the doorway, his recent meal cleared his throat.

Dropping to his knees, Reed continued to retch violently all over the boardwalk for one long minute. His insides twisted and turned, a pain flooding him like nothing he had ever experienced before. After a final, violent retch, he dropped face first onto the boardwalk next to what had been his lunch. He gasped for the air he had lost during the episode, his chest rising and falling rapidly.

After he was sure he had stabilized himself, he sat up on his knees, casting a single glance at what he had vomited up… and, in his weakened form, almost fainted. The eggs, biscuits, and gravy, intermixed with a couple of gulps of coffee was not a pretty sight when outside of his stomach, but it was lime green substance that was mixed in with the rest that stunned Reed as well as the others who had gathered in the doorway to the diner behind him.

He gazed at the sight in shock, then teetered backward and collapsed onto the boardwalk, the brightly lit world spiraling into darkness.

JACK DRUMMOND

EIGHT

Quantico, Virginia
FBI Academy

Knowles was bearing down upon her, and Chase found that she was completely defenseless.

She was just a teacher there at the academy.

Her rank of special agent had been suspended when she turned her badge over to the assistant director in Washington, which meant that she was weaponless.

He took Chase by her collar.

With an upward thrust of his hand, he sent her reeling up to the ceiling.

The impact against the ceiling knocked the wind out of her, and the descent from the ceiling offered Knowles the opportunity to thrust a hard right into her stomach and hurling her into the opposite wall.

Chase slammed hard against the wall, then slumped to the floor.

She gasped for air as Knowles bore down on her yet again.

Her vision dancing in and out of

focus, Chase knew that she would not be able to get the upper hand.

Knowles already had that.

Knowles brought up his leg as if to thrust it into her face when a sound like several birds chirping stopped him from doing just that.

Instead, to Chase's surprise, he began jerking with every impact of the bullets being fired from the suppressed weapon.

Finally the chirps ceased, after what seemed like an eternity.

Knowles fell backward, half-catching himself on her desk before dropping the rest of the way to the floor where he lay motionless, a pool of blood beginning to build beneath him, streaming from the numerous wounds patterning his back and chest.

Chase stared at his body, still too dazed from the blow to respond. The next thing she knew, she felt someone taking her by the arm.

"Get up!" a cold, harsh voice growled.

She fought to stand up, the world around her a vortex of shapes and flashing lights that danced all about her vision like little stars of different colors. Suddenly someone was shaking her, not violently, but enough to jar her out of vertigo and bring her back into reality.

"Snap out of it, Agent Chase!" the voice barked.

Chase looked to her right, to see who was clutching her right arm.

Her jaw dropped when she saw the man in black standing next to her.

In one hand he clutched her arm; in the other he gripped a suppressed handgun. She did not know whether to give the man a half-chance to speak or to deliver one solid kick and take of running.

He was the man who had given them access to the room that was responsible for Reed's disappearance, the room responsible for the missing two weeks of her own life.

Her eyes locked onto the black lenses of the sunglasses the man wore, his own eyes completely shielded behind them.

Her first notion was to run, to get as far away from the man as possible.

But he had shot KnowLes before the latter could kill her…though whether his intentions were to kill her anyway, she did not know.

The sight of the handgun he carried, however, offered her more of an incentive to stay in her current position and wait for a better opportunity of escape.

"You," she breathed in exasperation, her head throbbing and her ribs and spine already beginning to ache.

"If you want to live, Agent Chase," he said quickly, "then come with me now."

"W-What?" Chase stammered. "Why?"

"I don't have time to explain right now. Come on!"

There came a sound from somewhere behind them, and they both wheeled around to see where Knowles had fallen.

To Chase's surprise, she found herself staring at the stirring body of a man who had no less than a half dozen metal slugs lodged into his chest.

As the dead man started to sit up, the man in black took one step forward, lifted the Glock, and fired off one more round.

This time, the bullet lodged itself into Knowles's skull, penetrating his cranium in a spray of blood that coated the wall to next to him.

Chase blinked once, her mind still

racing to register all that had taken place in the past few seconds. Why had Knowles tried to kill her? Why was the man in black there? Why… was any of what was happening actually happening?

"You're just going to have to trust me," the man said, turning back to her.

"But you just…"

"I know, Agent Chase! But if you ever want to see Malcolm Reed alive again, then I suggest that you come with me… NOW!"

Reed?

Alive?

Chase just stood there, gaping. Her head swiveled from the man in black to the blood-stained and bullet-riddled body of Greg Knowles. Her mouth moved, but no words came out.

"How?" she finally managed to say.

"He's been returned, just like you."

Returned?

Chase blinked, still trying to get a grip on all the information that was coming at her like a freight train. She just could not function fast enough. It had been months since she had been in the field, and her body had slowly begun to get out of shape.

Could she really trust the man in

black?

"Listen to me," he said quietly, "I know where your partner is. I can get you to him, but only if you come with me *right now*."

Chase hesitated, her mind racing, her head spinning.

She took one long look back at Knowles's body, then finally back up at the man in black. She drew one long, deep breath.

Then she muttered, "Let's go."

NINE

Cracking his sleep-sticky eyes open, Malcolm Reed found himself lying on his back, staring up at a sun-caked concrete ceiling. Dozens of cracks streaked across the concrete slab of roof, suggesting that the building in which he lay had been standing for quite some time. He was lying on a hard surface, not unlike a mattress but what fell more like box-springs than anything else.

Sunlight poured in through a window high in the wall over his head. When Reed cocked his head to one side to get a better look at the window, he noticed that the window was barred.

"You finally decide to get up?"

Reed turned his head to the right, looking past the metal bars set close together and extending from the ceiling all the way down to the floor. A man sat on the other side of them, behind an old, scarred desk and in a chair that looked to be even older than the desk. He was sitting with his arms folded, an unpleasant look on his scruffy face.

He appeared to be in his fifties, with very little gray hair on the sides of his head.

The brown uniform he wore was dusty and unkempt, yet the star on his breast pocket gleamed brightly when it was struck by the sunlight, glaring so much so that Reed turned away.

Too late.

He was already seeing stars dancing around his peripheral vision.

His back was stiff from lying down for an extended period of time. He honestly did not know how any major company could construct a bed as uncomfortable as this one. He winced slightly as he pushed himself up on to his elbows and then rolled his neck clockwise, counterclockwise, then clockwise again, stretching out the muscles.

"Where am I?" he muttered after a moment, squinting somewhat as he looked back over at the man sitting on the other side of what he had finally determined was the door to a cell.

"In jail," the man replied bluntly.

"Yeah," Reed replied with a hint of sarcasm evident in his voice, "I gathered that. But where?"

The man studied Reed for a long moment, his sullen, gray eyes glaring hard at him. "San Ysidro," he finally said, "New

Mexico."

"New Mexico…" Reed muttered, his voice trailing off.

How in God's name did he manage to get to New Mexico?

What in God's name was he even doing in New Mexico?

Why New Mexico?

Reed let out a low moan, though it sounded more like a gruff chuckle.

The man on the other side of the cell stood up and crossed the room to the cell where Reed was being held.

"That was quite a mess you left down at the diner," the man who now stood just inches away from the bars said.

Reed squinted at the badge he wore, saw that it read: *sheriff.*

"Sorry about that," he uttered.

"Left a lot of folks in a bad way."

"Yeah, well, I'm sorry about that, too."

The sheriff glared at him.

"I don't like your attitude," he growled.

"Well, sheriff," Reed said, easing himself back prostrate on the bed and staring up at the ceiling with his hands interlocked behind his head, "I'm not going to keep apologizing just because I upset somebody new every time I turn around."

"You'd just better be careful that you don't upset the wrong person," the sheriff retorted. "You got a name, mister?"

"Yeah. Do you?"

No reply.

Reed glanced over at the sheriff.

"Listen, boy," the sheriff said, his voice barely above a whisper, "they ain't nobody in this here town who knows where you came from or how you even got here. Now, I'm a mite curious as to how you just happened to show up myself. You just showing up with no real business or nothing... it just ain't helping your case at all. The people here ain't all excited to welcome you when you don't even have a name."

"My name is Malcolm Reed. I'm a special agent with the FBI, call it in and see if it's true."

"Well..." the sheriff said, in a tone that suggested mockery, "is that so?"

Suddenly Reed cursed himself, the words the man in black had left him with at the Atoka Research Facility still ringing in his ears: *...your government has betrayed you.*

All of a sudden he was wishing that he had not told the sheriff to call it in and confirm his statement.

"Special Agent Malcolm Reed, huh? Well, then, Agent Reed, if you really are who you say you are, then you wouldn't mind showing me some proof or a badge of some sorts then, would you?"

A badge?

Proof?

Reed half wanted to breathe a sigh of relief, but a part of him wished that he knew where his badge was. He reached for his pockets and felt around. Nothing. Well, he thought, at least now there was nothing to go on. His claim, which, really was not a claim seeing as how he truly was Malcolm Reed, a Special Agent with the FBI, now seemed void.

Without so much as a badge or a driver's license, the sheriff was far less likely to call the nearest Bureau office and confirm his identity.

But look where he was.

Had the man in black been lying when he had told Reed and Chase of the government's betrayal?

Chase!

That was something else.

"There wouldn't happen to be a woman who just… randomly showed up here like I did, would there?" Reed asked.

"No. You got an accomplice with you?"

"No, just…"

"I'm still waiting on that identification, by the way."

Reed closed his mouth. Chase was not there, according to what the sheriff had said. But he could also be lying, like the man in black could have been. But the sheriff had no reason to lie, therefore he probably was not.

But had the man in black been lying back in Alaska?

The last thing Reed remembered was being engulfed by the light.

He could remember hearing his partner calling out to him as the light consumed them both.

And now he found himself in New Mexico, with a part of him missing. An emptiness. A void inside of his very soul.

"There is no proof," he said quietly

after several moments of silence.

"Just what I figured," the sheriff replied. "Might as well start talking. You're going to be in here until you decide to start doing just that."

JACK DRUMMOND

TEN

Quantico, Virginia

She was shaking by the time they had made it out of the academy through a private entrance, and Chase was still trying to calm herself even as they sped away from the academy in the black Ford. She still did not know why she had agreed to go along with the man's asinine claim.

How could he possibly know where Malcolm Reed was unless he himself had a hand in her partner's disappearance in the first place?

She looked at the man behind the wheel of the vehicle that was speeding down Fuller Road, toward the gated entrance to the Marine Corps base where the FBI Academy was located. She opened her mouth to speak when a high-pitched tone came from inside the man in black's dark overcoat. Chase jumped at the sound, still obviously shaken by the events that had unfolded just minutes before.

The man in black did not seem to notice her being startled, but instead retrieved his ringing cellular phone from inside his coat. In one smooth motion he flipped the phone open and brought it up to his ear. "Yeah?"

Chase could not hear what was being said by the individual... or individuals... on the other end of the line, even as she strained her ear.

"No," the man in black said into the phone, "he got to her first."

The gate entrance came into view, but was still a good piece up the road. The gate was down, and Chase began to wonder just how they were going to make it out of the base in one piece. Surely the man in black did not have clearance to a Marine Corps base...

"No. She's fine. I have her. Right."

The man in black closed the phone and replaced it inside his overcoat. Chase looked over at him curiously.

"What's going on?" she snapped.

No reply.

Chase looked forward, the gate entrance drawing ever closer.

It was still closed.

The guard would usually have already been standing out by now, ready to check and ensure that they had the correct papers and had permission to be coming and going.

Would she be tried for the murder of the man back in her office at the academy?

He had initially attacked her, but there was no witness to say otherwise.

And she was not even the one to kill him. But it was common knowledge that she was under investigation by the very people for which she worked. The odds for the situation at hand were *not* in her favor…

"Just how do you plan on getting out of here?" she asked, looking back over at the man.

Still, he offered no response.

They drew closer and closer to the gate, but the vehicle did not slow. In fact, Chase was sure that the man had pressed his foot even harder against the accelerator. They drew so close to the gate that she fought to scream at the man to slow down.

At the last possible second before what she was sure would have been a fatal head-on collision, the gate suddenly snapped open, and the vehicle blazed out of the newly made passageway.

Chase breathed a short sigh of relief, then turned her attention back to the man behind the wheel.

"Look," she said, gathering herself and delivering her words much more forcefully now, "I don't know who you are or what you want, but you asked me to trust you, and that's taking a whole lot of work on my part right now, especially after Alaska."

The man did not respond, but Chase knew that he could hear her... and was sure that he was listening.

"You told me you knew where Malcolm Reed is. Was that just another lie?"

A moment's silence.

Then...

"No."

"Then I want you to take me to him. Now."

"I'm sorry, Agent Chase, but now is not possible."

"I don't understand. Back there, you told me that this was my only chance at seeing him alive again. Now you're not going to take me to him?"

The man in black chortled a little.

"If only it were that simple," he muttered.

This was beyond idiotic.

"Look," Chase said, using her tone of voice to thrust the word at the man as if it were a spear, "I want you to take me to Malcolm Reed right now."

"I don't like to repeat myself. That is not possible."

"Then make it possible!"

"I can't!"

ChasE cursed, slammed herself back into her seat. She folded her arms, wanting to kick her feet and scream like a child.

She wanted to get to Malcolm Reed.

But obviously there was too much tension in the car at the moment, and there was no way she was going to get through to the man in black right then. She drew a breath, decided to drop the forceful attitude.

"The man back there," she said softly, "why was he trying to kill me?"

The man in black glanced over at her, then turned his attention back to the road.

"He said he was from the Department of Defense," she went on to say. "But he wasn't, was he?"

"No."

"Then why did he try to kill me?"

"The man that you encountered was after something that you do not possess but bore witness to."

"What would I have witnessed that

would make someone want to kill me?"

"He was after something that I have."

"Something that…"

What on earth could he have that she bore witness?

Then, it hit her like a freight train plowing into her stomach.

She suddenly felt nauseous.

"That… *thing*," she brought herself to say after a moment. "From the facility in Alaska."

The man in black did not speak, but instead offered her a curt nod.

"Of course," she said, her voice almost a whisper as she spoke more to herself than to the man next to her. "I saw you take it…but what is it?"

The man in black spared her a quick glance.

"It's complicated," he said dryly. "That's what it is."

"But it's obviously complicated enough to give someone a reason to want to have me killed," Chase retorted. "So I think I have a right to know just what in God's name someone wants to have me killed over."

He spared her another brief glance,

then turned his eyes back to the road ahead. He merged in with the rest of the traffic heading south on I-95, toward Richmond, Virginia.

"It's an extraterrestrial biological entity," he said finally, "that's been on this planet for centuries."

An... *extraterrestrial biological entity*?

Chase almost laughed.

"What're you saying," she said, "that it's some kind of... alien?"

The man in black looked at her, and she could feel his cold, hard eyes piercing her through the lenses of the dark sunglasses he wore.

"Agent Chase," he said, "that's *exactly* what I'm saying."

JACK DRUMMOND

ELEVEN

San Ysidro, New Mexico

After the sheriff had made a few other threatening remarks, he went back behind his desk and set to work on some papers. He started humming as he worked, and several occasions Reed was tempted to tell the man to shut up, as he could not carry a tune in a bucket.

But Reed decided it best to keep his mouth shut.

The ultra-thin thread of tension in the jail at the time could have been cut with the dullest of knives.

The minutes ticked by slowly.

The sheriff's humming was badly off-tune and threatened to make Reed's ears bleed. Reed continued to stare up at the cracked ceiling of the jail cell, pondering the past.

His past.

There was no way of telling the time, but it was a good hour before there was any change in the status quo of the tiny jail.

That change came when the front door, which was located all the way on the opposite side of the small jail from the cell, opened and Reed looked over to see the young boy to whom he had returned the soccer ball.

Their eyes met when the boy saw Reed.

For the longest of moment's they held each other's gaze. Like a gateway into the boy's emotions, Reed could see fear, contempt, and pity in the boy's eyes.

"What is it, Toby?" the sheriff growled suddenly.

The boy immediately turned away from Reed to look at the sheriff.

"It's Mr. Wilson," the boy said quickly. "He's down at the bar and is causing some trouble with Mrs. Lenore."

"Wilson, eh? Probably drunk again."

The sheriff stood, taking up the shotgun that was propped up against the wall next to his desk. He started across the room in the direction of the door, but stopped in his tracks after just a couple of seconds and looked through the metal bars of the jail cell at Reed, who still lay on the bed, as comfortable-looking as he could have possibly been. The sheriff then looked down at the boy.

"Toby," he said, "I want you to stay here and watch this man. Don't talk to him, and don't even listen to him if he talks to you. Just watch him. If he tries to get out or anything, you just come running and get me. Do you understand?"

The boy looked up at the sheriff, then over at Reed. He then looked back at the sheriff.

"Do you understand," the sheriff repeated, only more harshly this time.

"Yes, sir," the boy muttered timidly after a moment's hesitation.

The sheriff looked at the boy a moment longer, then turned and crossed the room to the door on the other side. He pushed it open and stepped out onto the boardwalk, letting the door slide shut behind him; leaving only Reed and the boy named Toby standing inside.

As the door closed behind the sheriff, Reed watched as Toby looked up and over at him. He held the boy's gaze for several seconds before Toby turned away and crossed the room to sit down in the sheriff's chair behind the old desk. The boy spun around in the old chair several times, without even so much as acknowledging

Reed's presence in the cell across the room.

"Hey," Reed finally spoke up as he watched the boy.

Toby seemed not to hear him, as he went on spinning round in the sheriff's chair.

"Hey," Reed repeated, "Toby."

The boy glanced his way at the mention of his own name.

"You don't need to be afraid of me," Reed said, setting his tone of voice to be as reassuring to the boy as possible.

No response from Toby, but the boy did stop spinning in the chair and stared hard at Reed through the metal bars of his cell.

"Look," Reed went on, "I didn't do anything wrong. I'm a police officer, to be honest. Thing is, I don't even know what I'm doing here."

Toby Studied Reed for a long time, apparently trying to determine whether or not he should even contemplate listening to Reed.

"Can you help me, Toby?"

Nothing.

"Can you tell me how I got here?"

The boy hesitated, then spoke up. "I'm not supposed to talk to you."

"I know, Toby. I heard what he said.

But c'mon. You have to help me out a little here. Have you ever seen me before now?"

Toby went back to spinning around in the chair. "There were some men who brought you here a couple nights ago."

Men?

"What men? What were they doing?"

"I'm not supposed to talk about it."

Reed inclined his head at the boy's last statement. "Now who told you not to talk about it?"

"The men who brought you here. They took you to Mr. Haggerty's motel here in town and left you there. They told us not to talk to you about anything."

That was disturbing in and of itself. But then, the boy's sudden cooperation begged a particular question…

"Why are you telling me now?" Reed asked after a moment.

"Because you said you're a police officer. That means if they were hurting you, they must be bad men, doesn't it?"

Well, that was pretty good logic. Smart kid. But…

"They were *hurting* me?"

Toby stopped spinning in mid-turn and drifted the rest of the way to a stop so that he could face Reed. He nodded. "That's what you said."

Wait… what?

"What I said?"

The boy nodded again. "When they brought you here, you were saying, don't let them hurt me anymore, don't let them hurt me anymore."

Had that really happened? Had Reed actually been aware of what they were doing to him just a couple of nights ago? Possibly. He did not know. And those men that the boy was talking about… he could not recall having dealt with any such beings in the recent past.

"They said that you were in a car accident," Toby said, "that you were just dreaming, that they weren't really hurting you."

Had it been a car accident?

No. Surely not.

A car accident was too ludicrous.

He would remember that, wouldn't he?

"Do you remember anything else, Toby?"

The boy looked hard in thought for a long moment, then looked back at Reed. "I remember that the men said they worked for the government."

JACK DRUMMOND

TWELVE

Richmond, Virginia

The many charitable churches and feeding centers that were located in the area drew many homeless citizens to Monroe Park. As Elizabeth Chase looked about her from her position in the passenger seat of the black Ford sedan, she counted nearly a dozen people wandering aimlessly about.

Nowhere to go… probably no family either.

The man in black was gone from the driver's seat. He had pulled the vehicle off to the shoulder, ordered Chase to stay put, climbed out of the vehicle, and disappeared into the park. Chase was left alone in the cab of the Ford, the vehicle rocking gently with every passing car. She was tempted to get out and start running away from the park, to put some distance between herself and the man in black before he returned. But he insisted that he knew of Malcolm Reed's location, and that was really the only thing that kept Chase glued to her seat, fidgeting nervously.

Ten minutes passed, and Chase began

to wander whether or not the man in black was even going to return. He had offered her no explanation as to where he was going, nor told her how long he would be gone. He just expected her to trust him and do exactly as he said.

Ironic.

It was the man in black himself who had left Reed and her at the Atoka Research Facility with the parting words: *trust no one.*

And now he wanted her to trust him, while he gave her no reassurance, and very little incentive to do what he expected of her. Yet It was that small incentive, the claim of knowing where Malcolm Reed was, that held her in the passenger seat of the Ford, wondering, hoping that she was not being set up. Any number of things could happen to her while she sat there.

He could just be abandoning her.

The car could be wired with a bomb so that when she attempted to get out she would be killed in the ensuing explosion.

The mental list she had made went on and on. Yet she remained seated, doing what the man in black asked of her. For six months she had dedicated every waking spare moment of her time to trying to track down her partner's location. And the thought also occurred to her, that though Reed was missing, she, too, had been missing for a total of two weeks' time. Those missing two weeks of her own life haunted her. She had attempted to access those misted memories, but to no avail. Somehow she hoped that by finding Reed, she would also find the key to unlocking her own memories...

Perhaps, by finding Reed, she could access those missing two weeks of her life and find out how...why...she had managed to return to her home in Washington, D.C., and wake up in her own bed two weeks later with no recollection of how she had gotten there.

But then there was also the issue of the man in black.

Who was he?

She had seen the man for less than two whole minutes, six months before, just moments before she lost all recollection of what occurred just two weeks after that... just moment before her partner had disappeared. She speculated that he knew more than he was letting on, yet the reticence of the man himself and the aftershock of what had occurred at the FBI academy in Quantico had prohibited her from thinking straight.

But now that she found herself alone, she allowed herself time to gather her thoughts. There were so many questions.

And she needed answers.

Even if he could not answer them all, she *knew* that the man in black could answer some of them.

She turned and looked out of the passenger window. Her eyes were heavy, and she could have gone to sleep right there, were it not for the adrenaline pumping through her veins.

At this point, her anxiety had overcome her exhaustion.

Her peripheral vision picked up movement, and she turned quickly to see the driver's side door open and the man in black climb inside. He carried with him a manila folder, which he handed to her.

"Where did you go?" she asked as she flipped the folder open, revealing two airline tickets.

"I had to meet someone."

"To get tickets?"

"I told you I couldn't get you to your partner."

"You had to get airline tickets?"

"Well, we could drive to New Mexico if you'd like," the man retorted, starting up the engine and pulling out onto the street.

Chase looked over at him.

New Mexico…

JACK DRUMMOND

THIRTEEN

San Ysidro, New Mexico

Your government has betrayed you...

Those words continued to play over and over in Reed's mind as the boy looked at him curiously. Slowly, Reed sat up on the hard bed.

"Toby, are you sure that they were from the government?"

The boy nodded quickly.

"They had badges," he said.

"Badges?"

"Yeah, and their badges had the letters F, B, and I on them."

FBI?

Reed muttered a curse to himself.

"So they took me to the motel... then what?"

"They left."

"They left?"

The boy nodded.

"They just... *left*?"

"Yep."

Reed chewed his bottom lip as he thought.

Suddenly the door opened, and the

sheriff re-entered, alone.

"Thanks, Toby," the sheriff said without looking at Reed, "you can go."

Toby looked back at Reed, then hopped out of the chair and sprinted out the door. When he had gone, the sheriff turned and closed the door. He then proceeded over to his desk and leaned the shotgun up against the wall. He sat down and began shuffling through some papers. After a couple of minutes, he glanced up at Reed, who sat upright on the stiff bed.

"What's eating at you?" the sheriff spoke.

"Huh?" Reed said, snapping out of his thoughts.

"Something's eatin' at you. What is it?"

"Oh, well, I'm still trying to figure out what I did to get thrown in here."

"You're a suspicious person with a refusal to cooperate with the law."

"Refusal to cooperate?"

The sheriff nodded. "You won't tell me where you came from," he said, "or how you got here or…"

"How am I supposed to tell you what I don't know?" Reed interjected.

The sheriff eyed him for a long moment.

"Be careful, son," the sheriff said, "that mouth of yours is going to get you in more trouble than you're worth."

"Me? Sheriff, I think it's time that you did some explaining yourself."

"Come again?"

"You heard me," Reed said, his voice rising, "it's time for you to do some talking."

"What do you mean, boy?"

"I mean that I want to know why you're not telling me everything. Why you're throwing me in here because of something that *you* know."

The sheriff glared at him.

"Son," the sheriff said, speaking very slow and seriously, "I think you'd better shut that mouth of yours before I have to come in there and do it myself."

"Who were those men that brought me here?"

"What?"

"The men with the FBI, the ones who brought me here. Who were they? Where did they come from?"

"Did that boy say something?"

Toby.

Crap.

He had not considered that Toby would take the blame for this.

Reed muttered a low curse.

"Was it the boy?" the sheriff boomed, rising out of his seat.

"I can remember," Reed said suddenly.

The sheriff stared at him for a long moment, then turned and started for the front door.

"I knew I shouldn't have left him alone with you," he muttered as he neared the door.

"No," Reed said, now fearful for Toby's sake, "wait!"

But the sheriff kept going, and an instant later disappeared through the front door. The door slammed shut, leaving Reed behind in the cell, staring after the sheriff. He stood and cursed again, kicking across the cell the bucket that was catching water droplets from the numerous cracks in the ceiling.

Probably a leak in the plumbing.

For a moment silence fell, the weight of it seeming to press down upon Reed's shoulders like thousands of gallons of water.

Then the silence was broken… by the sound of metal grinding metal.

Reed looked up at the bars in the window, only to see a small string coated with metal filings cutting into them. He glanced back at the front door, then stood up on the bed so that he was eye-level with the bars.

On the other side of the window was an old man, dark-skinned, but definitely not as much so as an African American. No, Reed was sure the old man was a Native American of some sort, and the feather the old man had in his hair more or less confirmed Reed's suspicions.

"What're you doing?" Reed asked quickly. "Who are you?"

The old man continued to cut the metal bars with the string coated in metal filings. He glanced down at Reed, but offered no response. INstead, he worked even faster and more furiously. A couple of seconds later the first bar fell out of place, and the old man set to work on the second.

Whoever he was, Reed could not see why the old man would want to come into the jail cell. But if the old man could get those bars out of the way, then it left him

with an opportunity.
An opportunity to escape.

FOURTEEN

Sandston, Virginia

When the man in black had presented the airline tickets to the woman at the front desk at Richmond International Airport, he and Chase were boarded on a first-class charter in minutes. Within a half-hour of arriving, they were taking off. As the plane sped down the runway, Chase watched as the airport and the other planes streaked by at an increasingly alarming rate.

The private plane that they had so suddenly boarded was rather small and the only passengers on board were Chase and the man in black. He sat on the other side of the aircraft, looking out of his own window. A moment later the nose of the plane tilted skyward, and then they were off the runway and into the air.

For several minutes there was silence between the two of them as the plane ascended higher into the sky and the vehicles and such far below grew smaller and smaller until they were obscured by the clouds.

Chase finally looked over at the man

in black. "Where are we going?"

"Albuquerque," he replied dryly.

"Is that where Agent Reed is?"

"No."

"Then why--"

"Because where he is, there is no airport. He's about fifty miles north of Albuquerque, in a town called San Ysidro."

"Never heard of it."

"It's a small village. The people there are nice enough, but it's a place that the government has had under surveillance for some time now, ever since the place became a known beacon for abduction cases."

"Abductions? You're talking as in alien abductions?"

"Essentially, yes."

Alien abductions…

Did he really take her for an idiot?

"You never told me what you did with that thing from the facility," she said after a moment, looking over at the man in black.

"I destroyed it."

"Really?"

"Yes."

"Why?"

"Because it was what I had been instructed to do."

"Were you instructed to kill Alan Donovan?"

Silence.

She knew that she must have struck a nerve.

The man in black looked over at her, but she did not back down. No, she instead held his gaze firmly.

"I did what I had been instructed to do."

"Do you always do what you're instructed?"

The man in black turned his head to look back out the window, seemingly trying to ignore her. But she pressed on, determined to get some answeRs out of him.

"Were you instructed to send Agent Reed and me into that room? Do you know where I was for the two weeks following that incident?"

No response.

Now he was ignoring her, and she was beginning to grow tired of not having answers.

"Answer me!"

The man in black looked up and over at her. For a moment he looked as though he were going to cross the plane and slap her hard.

But he restrained himself.

"Agent Chase, I'll tell you what you want to know," he said finally. "But if anyone discovers what I've told you, then they will do everything in their power to make sure that you don't walk back into Washington alive."

"I want to know," Chase said as firmly as ever. "Now."

"Fine."

"Let's start with a name. Surely you've got one."

"Job."

"Job?"

"Yes. My name is Job."

FIFTEEN

San Ysidro, New Mexico

The second and third bars were out just minutes later, and the old man set to work on the fourth and final bar. Reed glanced back at the front door of the jail cell, expecting the sheriff to reenter at any moment.

"Look," he said, turning back to the old man, "why are you doing this?"

"You cannot die here," the old man said quickly in a dry, almost rasping voice.

He was not making much sense.

Then again, Reed thought, nothing was making much sense.

The fourth bar fell out of place, and Reed stuck his head through the newly opened hole in the wall. The old man stepped down off the ladder on which he stood and motioned for Reed to follow him. Reed glanced back at the door to the sheriff's office, hesitated, then scrambled out of the window. Just as his feet touched the ladder and he started down, he heard the front door open, and an instant later heard the sheriff scream a curse.

"We must go!" the old man hissed.

Reed dropped from midway up the ladder and hit the sun-baked ground running. The old man was surprisingly fast for his age, and both he and Reed sprinted for a truck that was sitting at the bottom of the small sand hill which lay behind the jail. Reed lost his footing starting down the hill, rolled the rest of the way to the bottom, then stood and rushed for the truck. He jumped into the passenger seat and a moment later the old man was climbing into the driver's seat.

As the old man cranked the key already in the ignition, Reed glanced back up at the sand hill and saw the sheriff emerge at the top, his shotgun in hand. The engine roared to life, drowning out the sheriff's order to stop. The old man dropped the truck into gear and punched the accelerator. The truck's tires spun for a moment in the sand; then the adhesive friction of the tires grinding into the surface on which it sat took hold, and the truck burst forward and raced across the desert.

The blast of the sheriff's shotgun was only just loud enough, and a spray of dirt kicked up near the truck's right front tire. Reed shielded his eyes from the wall of dirt and grit, and an instant later the old man drove the truck up onto the two-lane road leading out of the small village.

A sign on the shoulder of the road raced by, and Reed glimpsed the words **HIGHWAY 44** written on the sign, with an arrow pointing the same direction in which they were going. Reed glanced at the old man, whose sharp eyes flicked up at the rearview.

"Who are you?" Reed asked.

"My name is Tucson," the old man said.

"Where are you taking me?"

"I live on the Zia Indian Reservation near here. That is where we are going."

"A reservation? That's government owned."

Tucson nodded. "Yes it is."

"Why did you help me back there?"

"Because you must not die."

"I wasn't going to die in jail. I was probably as safe there as anywhere."

Tucson glared at him. "What did he tell you?"

"The sheriff?"

Tucson nodded again.

"Nothing. But I was told that I was

brought to the town by government agents."

Reed was sure he saw a dry smile cross the old man's dried and cracked lips.

"Do you recall how you came to the town?" Tucson asked.

Reed thought for a moment. "No."

Tucson said nothing, but pressed his foot down a little further on the accelerator. "They will be looking for you."

"So the government did bring me here?"

"My friend," Tucson said, speaking softly but in that same crispy voice as before, "there Is much that you do not know. You will get your answers, but not now. Not yet."

"Why not now?"

"There is much you must understand before you can come to understand your purpose."

"My...*what*?"

The old man looked at Reed and smiled softly.

The rest of the way to the reservation, there was little talk between the two of them.

SIXTEEN

Zia Indian Reservation
Sandoval County, New Mexico

They had passed through several villages after entering reservation territory and had not stopped at a single one. They had instead cut onto a dirt trail off the main roadway where the truck finally rumbled to a halt just outside a large pueblo, a dwelling cutaway in the side of a nearby cliff. There was no way for Reed to find the time, as the truck's clock was too dim to read. But judging by the way the sun was hanging in the cloudless sky, hovering above the distant mountains that were extending ever so elegantly toward the heavens.

"Where are we?" Reed asked as Tucson cut off the engine.

"My home," the old man replied, opening the driver's side door and stepping out onto the sun-baked sand.

Tucson slammed the door and started around the front of the truck. Reed sat for a moment watching him, then reluctantly opened the door and climbed out. Closing the door behind him, he followed Tucson over to the pueblo, glancing about him as he went.

There was nothing but the desert in every direction he looked. The distortions of hot and cool air waves made the distant mountains dance in strange, misleading ways.

Why was he there?

What did the old man want with him?

Tucson thrust open the door, a slab of wood that looked more like a chunk of bark taken from a tree than anything else. But there were no trees nearby, only the occasional shrub or cactus.

Tucson stepped inside.

Reed, though a little reluctant, then followed after him. After entering, Tucson closed the door behind him and crossed the room to a small fireplace. He added several smaller twigs as well as two larger pieces of wood to what few embers were still glowing within the fireplace.

Reed watched him for a long moment.

Why on earth would he be *adding* fuel to the fire in the middle of the desert?

Flames began to catch to the wood Tucson added to the fireplace, and Reed shed the long-sleeved shirt he wore in favor of the thin, plain white t-shirt he wore underneath. Tucson drew back from the fireplace and glanced over at Reed, who was draping his shirt over the back of a handmade wicker chair sitting near him.

"Keep that close by," Tucson said, nodding toward the shirt. "Nights here can grow cold."

Reed glanced down at the shirt then back up at the old man. He gave a brisk nod as Tucson stood and crossed the room. He brushed past Reed and yanked open the door to a small refrigerator in the corner of the pueblo.

"You have electricity here?" Reed said.

"It's all underground. The storms and winds can be dangerous to any type of power line and the government doesn't want to have their property destroyed by nature."

"The government?"

Tucson emerged from the refrigerator with two cans of soda pop. He passed one can to Reed, who took it from him and popped the tab. He took a long drink of the cool liquid.

"Yes," Tucson said, popping the tab of his own can of soda. "This is government-owned property."

"Then why did you bring me here if you want to help me?"

"We've been through this already. What did they tell you back there in the town?"

Reed studied the lines of the old man's face for a long time. His own face began to tingle. His jaw began to grow numb. "Government agents. They were the ones who took me to the town."

"A lie," Tucson said quickly.

Now the entire right side of Reed's face went numb. His vision began to contort in strange ways, the old man's shape suddenly Changed to a tall, slender figure no thicker than the width of a toothpick. His mind seemed to be going numb to the world around him.

"What's happening to me?" Reed moaned, suddenly finding himself dizzy.

His fingers went limp, and the can slipped from his weakened grip. He dropped into the chair over which he had draped his shirt, his hands trembling, nerves contracting spastically.

"Do not worry," Tucson said quietly, his voice almost a whisper. "It is only to help you relax."

Reed tried to speak, but his throat felt as though it was closing off. His tongue was heavy, and a moment later he was not even sure if it was still contained inside of his mouth. He tried to stand from the chair. His legs were numb. He pitched forward, caught himself momentarily on the table.

Then his arms gave way and he toppled over onto the floor, his world spiraling into darkness.

JACK DRUMMOND

SEVENTEEN

Malcolm Reed awoke to a darkened sky, a coldness that he had never before experienced, and a feeling of numbness to the world around him the likes of which he had never before felt. Tucson was standing nearby, and Reed turned his head slightly so that he could see the old man who was striking rock against rock in an attempt to start a fire.

"Where am I?" Reed muttered.

Tucson looked up and over at him as he tried to sit up. "No," Tucson hissed quietly. "You must lie still. The spirits are not here yet."

"The...*what*?"

"The spirits are not here yet. They must choose you!"

Reed fought the blankets off and stood. He was shirtless, and as he stood he suddenly realized he was standing in the middle of the desert in utter darkness. He wondered how Tucson could see him, as he could barely make out the outline of the old man in the darkness.

"Lie back down," Tucson said. "You must wait for the spirits!"

"Look," Reed said, "I'm tired of playing all these stupid games with people! Where am I and how did I get here? Who are you and why did you bring me here?"

"They are here!"

"Who? The spirits?"

"Yes!"

"That's bull--"

The force of the impact slamming into his chest knocked Reed flat onto his back and left him fighting for air.

"Lie still," Tucson said from his position next to the fire that he suddenly managed to start, "unless the spirits take you."

"Take me?" Reed gasped, "What hit me?"

Tucson did not respond, but instead stared into the fire for a long time. Reed lay there, trying to determine whether or not there was a supernatural force at work there or if old man Tucson was just flat out crazy.

After a long time, Tucson said, "Alright, my friend. You must come to me."

"What?"

"Come, quick!"

Reed stood slowly and approached the old man, who sat with his legs crossed and feet under him, his arms folded, also shirtless. Reed sat next to him and looked into the fire, welcoming the warmth in the cold of the desert night around him.

"Look at me," Tucson said.

Reed looked up and over at Tucson, pulling his knees close to himself and gripping his shins with his Hands. It was far too cold to be in the desert at night without a shirt. Suddenly Tucson reached forward and placed his fingers on Reed's temples.

"Hey," Reed exclaimed, "what're you doing?"

"Quiet," Tucson muttered. "Close your eyes."

"What?"

"Do it!"

With a sigh of irritation, Reed closed his eyes.

For a long time he sat there, not sure of what was happening. After a time, Tucson removed his fingers.

"Can I open them?" Reed said.

"Yes," Tucson said quietly.

Reed blinked his eyes open, and suddenly found that they were not alone.

Instead, they were surrounded by no less than thirty Native Americans, all of them seemingly unaware of Reed's and Tucson's presence amongst them.

"Now," Tucson said to Reed, "you will know the truth."

EIGHTEEN

Albuquerque, New Mexico

No luggage allowed for a quick and decisive trip out of the airport. Outside, the man who had identified himself to Chase as Job hailed a cab into which they both climbed. The cabby was a quiet fellow, soft spoken. He employed nothing more than the radio to fill the awkward silence that had befallen the cab the moment Job had given the cabby directions.

Chase was quiet.

She bit her bottom lip tightly as she stared out the window in deep thought. She pondered all that Job had told her on the plane. The truth, which Job so applicably called the information he had imparted to her, was far from anything that Chase herself could have thought up or could have ever deemed herself possible of doing so.

An ongoing government conspiracy…

Clandestine Russian experiments…

The truth about the man who had attacked her in Quantico and the creature from the Atoka Research Facility…

The truth about all those who had

117

accompanied them to Alaska, including Agent Donovan…

And where she herself had been for two weeks' time…where her partner, Malcolm Reed, had been for six months…

It was all something that she would expect from a television show such as *The X-Files* or from a science fiction novel.

Soon they had left the city of Albuquerque behind and headed out on the main roadway, driving into the desert. The darkness of the New Mexico night closed in around them, encasing the cab and pressing forcefully against the windows. At one point Chase's hand tapped the window lightly, and a chill shot up her arm. She shuttered at the thought of where her partner was and what he had gone through.

"Hey," the cab driver muttered after a moment, "what is that?" he said, nodding forward.

Chase inclined her head around the passenger seat and looked out through the windshield. In the middle of the road, silhouetted against the deep blue of the night sky vaguely illuminated by the incandescent moon, was what appeared to be the figure of a man. She felt Job adjust himself slightly so that he could get a better view as well.

"Keep going!" Job said suddenly.

Chase looked over at him through the darkened interior of the cab. "What?"

"Don't stop."

"Hey," the cabby began, sounding unsure of what he was being told to do. "Look, I..."

In a blur of motion, Job drew a handgun from the inside of his coat and pressed the barrel against the back of the cabby's skull.

"What are you doing?" Chase screamed. "I didn't come all this way just so you could kill an innocent civilian!"

"Keep going," Job shouted.

The cabby's foot fell against the accelerator, and Chase felt the cab picking up speed.

The man standing in the road did not seem to care, but stood firm, directly in the cab's path. Chase watched, jaws set tightly, teeth clenched, her hands drawn into tight fists, as the car rocketed toward the man in the road, gaining speed with every passing second.

They grew close enough so that the headlights fell upon the figure standing in the road, and for an instant Chase thought that she recognized the face of the man in the cab's path. And in that instant she doubted herself, doubted her own eyes. She even doubted her own sanity.

A moment later the cab slammed hard into the man. His body rolled up onto the hood of the car, the force of the impact sending a crack streaking across the windshield. He rolled across the windshield and up over the roof before bouncing off the trunk and onto the pavement below.

"Stop the car," Job said once the man had returned to the surface of the pavement.

The way the nervous cabby slammed on the brakes, Chase thought that she could very well have gone through the windshield were it not for the seatbelt she wore. When the car had come to a screeching halt, Job passed her the handgun.

"Watch him," Job said, then he opened the door and climbed out.

Chase held the gun on the cabby with shaking hands.

"Please," the cabby said, "please, I have a wife and--"

"Shut up," Chase hissed. "I won't do anything to you, but I'm not so sure about him. He's out of his mind."

She chanced a glance out of the rear windshield, watched as Job made his way over to where the body of the man they had hit lay. She squinted hard, trying to see just what the man in black was doing when he knelt down next to the body.

Suddenly there was movement from the front of the cab, and Chase whipped her head around in time to see the cabby clearing the driver's seat and start sprinting on down the road. She kicked her own door open and jumped out. She pointed the handgun over the roof of the cab and shouted, "Freeze!"

She squeezed off a round that went whining out into the distant night. The cabby stopped dead in his tracks not thirty feet from the front of the cab.

"Agent Chase!"

She glanced over her shoulder, barely able to make out the darkling form of Job, whom she suspected was looking at her. She honestly did not know how he managed to see her. He had not taken off those sunglasses.

"It's okay," she said, turning back to the cabby, who stood with his hands in the air, trembling, "I'm with the FBI. I'm not going to hurt you. Just turn around and come back to the car."

"How do I know you're not lying?" the cabby managed to say.

"Agent Chase!" Job shouted again, sounding a bit more frantic this time.

"Because I have a badge," Chase said, ignoring the man in black. "Now come back to the car and you can see it."

Suddenly, the back windshield of the cab shattered, and Chase jumped aside in fright. Job was wedged in between the roof and the trunk of the cab, half of him having disappeared inside the cab itself.

She looked back in the direction from which he was thrown.

The Man they had hit was standing.

And he was walking toward her.

NINETEEN

Zia Indian Reservation

"It is ancient Zia tradition," Tucson said quietly, though Reed could not understand why the old man was whispering, as it was fairly obvious that the Indians dancing about with their drums and rattles were unaware of their presence. "The Zia would offer up their own to the kachinas, the spirits that lived amongst them but who fled to the skies when craving attention."

"Okay," Reed said slowly. "So what is this? A kachinas festival or something?"

"Yes."

"Over there," Tucson said, nodding toward an old man in a feather headdress who was sitting at the center of a circle formed by a group of elder Zia, "that's the chief of this tribe."

The dancing and pounding of drums continued for several minutes more. Reed looked all about him at the Zia as they went about their festival. He wondered how he had gotten there and what Tucson had to do with it. And what had Tucson meant by *the truth?*

Suddenly the drums ceased and the dancing stopped. The Zia who were standing dropped to their knees, folding their legs and turning their eyes upon the chief. The chief immediately began to a chant in a language unfamiliar to Reed, who, nonetheless, listened as intently as ever.

"The kachinas look in favor of our small gathering," Tucson translated the chief's words, whispering softly off to Reed's left. "They wish to inhabit several of you once more. But who shall have this honor?"

Every Zia there broke out in a foreign babble that to Reed was gibberish. Presently, the chief lifted his hand and began to speak again, his voice raspy and old.

"Silence," Reed heard Tucson whisper from somewhere behind him. "The kachinas themselves will decide."

At the chief's command, silence fell upon the gathered Zia, and only the popping and crackling of the large fire at their center was to be heard. After a moment, the chief broke out into a subtle chant, and a minute later was joined by the rest of the tribe, all of them chanting in unison. Reed waited impatiently for Tucson to translate what they were saying, but no such words came. Finally he turned to look at Tucson. "What're they saying?"

"This," Tucson said, "I do not know."

Suddenly a blinding white light exploded in the sky above them.

It was a luminescent, glowing force that shattered the night with such force that Reed was knocked off his haunches and flat onto his back. He stared up at the light that was quickly expanding across the sky as the chants of the Zia grew louder and more frantic.

"Tucson," Reed called as he scrambled to his feet, "what's going on?"

The old man offered no response, but instead remained crouched as he stared up at the white light. Reed looked up at the white light as well, a cold, hard realization suddenly flooding back to him.

The Atoka Research Facility…

The white light…

Chase…

The white light grew larger and seemed to be falling down upon the Zia who stood and chanted in unison, as though it were one massive luminescent blanket drifting silently down from the night sky. Reed sprinted into the midst of the Zia and attempted to shove the first one he came to out of the way. With his hands outstretched, he approached the Zia and pressed against the man's chest. To his utter shock, his hands passed through the Zia's chest and emerged from the man's back.

The blanket of light grew closer to the gathered Zia, and Reed took notice of Tucson, who had finally stood and was shielding his eyes from the light.

"Tucson!" Reed screamed, "Help me!"

As the blanket of light fell upon the Zia, a violent shaking that commenced, and a high-pitched whine came from the night itself.

Then the light exploded in all directions, sending an invisible shockwave that lifted Reed off his feet and hurled him over near to where Tucson stood. Dust smarted his eyes and burned his nostrils, and he landed hard on his back, the wind knocked out of him.

The entire Zia tribe was gone, along with the light.

Tucson remained standing, simply

shielding his eyes from the wall of dust that was kicked up by the shockwave. Reed clambered to his feet, gasping for air as he did so. He turned his back to the wall of dust as it encased him, his eyes slammed shut. After a moment the cloud dissipated, and he opened his eyes to find himself standing inside of the small pueblo Tucson had taken him to. Tucson was staring out of a small cutaway that acted as a window for the pueblo.

"Tucson," Reed exclaimed, "what…"

Tucson suddenly turned to face Reed, his once Old and sullen gray eyes now glowing a brilliant orange. "They're here."

JACK DRUMMOND

TWENTY

She did not know what effect it would have, but Chase lifted her handgun and fired off three rounds in rapid succession at the man walking toward her. He jerked with the impact of the two bullets that slammed into his chest, the third whining off into the night. Job moaned next to her, but Chase kept her focus on the man whom she had just shot.

"Get up," Chase whispered out of the corner of her mouth. "Get up, Job. Or we're never going to make it out of here."

The man suddenly regained his composure and continued toward them. As he drew closer, the moon briefly illuminated his face, and Chase gasped.

"My God!" she exclaimed.

She emptied the rest of the clip of the handgun at the man, several of the shots impacting his chest and knocking him a mere step or two back each time. This, however, was enough to allow Job sufficient time to groggily emerge from the car, his face cut, clothes torn, and glasses askew on his face. He reached inside of his torn overcoat and retrieved a small and oddly shaped syringe. The object was made of shiny silver metal that glinted in the starlight.

Knowles was only a few steps away from them now, and Job stepped in front of Chase and launched himself at Knowles. He attempted to jab the syringe into Knowles's neck, but Knowles extended his arm and managed to block the blow. He then extended his foot into Job's stomach, sending him reeling into the trunk of the cab.

The syringe fell from his limp fingers as he gasped for air.

Chase backed quickly away from the car, turned, and started off into the desert at a dead run. After a moment she chanced a glance back, only to find that Knowles was bearing down on top of her. She tried to scream for Job to help, but at that instant Knowles launched himself forward and tackled her to the ground. She landed hard with Knowles on top of her, and he turned her so that she lay on her back. She opened her mouth to scream, but suddenly found that she could not as Knowles wrapped both hands around her throat.

Again she tried to scream, fighting the

bigger man with every ounce of strength she could muster. She quickly realized that it was no use.

She began to feel herself fading.

She could not breathe, and stars began to dance in and out of her vision as she stared up into Knowles's badly bruised and butchered face.

An instant later Job appeared just behind Knowles, and he brought the syringe around so that it punctured Knowles's throat. His grip around Chase's neck loosened, and she heaved the man off of her, gasping for air. Blood spouted from Knowles's throat and trickled from his bottom lip. Chase massaged her raw throat as Job straddled Knowles and with a strong slap, drove the syringe even deeper into the man's neck.

Knowles gurgled and blood bubbled from the wound, soaking the saNd beneath him as the very life-light in the man's eyes began to fade. Chase watched in shock as Knowles heaved a final breath, and then stopped moving altogether. For a long moment she sat, staring at his lifeless body. She was wary of his true state, though, as she had just watched him consume an entire magazine of bullets that had neglected to even slow him down.

Presently she felt someone's hand grace her shoulder and she instinctively pulled away. She wheeled around to see Job standing next to her. He seemed to have regained his composure, though he appeared to favor his right leg while standing.

"It's all right," he said softly. "He's dead."

"H-how can you be sure?" Chase stammered.

"The syringe," Job said, gesturing toward the small metal object embedded in the side of Knowles's throat. "It's what I retrieved when we stopped in Richmond."

"But I thought you said you had someone to meet."

"I did. And I retrieved the syringe. Now we must go if we're going to make it to Reed in…" his voice trailed off.

"What is it?" Chase asked quietly, glancing around.

The cabby was missing.

Suddenly she heard a low hum emitting from somewhere above them. She looked up in time to be blinded by two white lights that suddenly illuminated them both in two separate pools of luminescence. Chase brought up her hand to shield her eyes from the light as she came to the realization that they were being targeted by two helicopters.

She felt Job grip her arm firmly and heard him shout, "Run!"

"But what about Reed?" Chase exclaimed as she fell into step behind him as he sprinted for the cab.

"It's too late! They have him!"

"Who?" Chase shouted over the roar of the helicopter blades that grew increasingly louder as the choppers descended from the night skies.

"The government!"

Job circled the cab and dived into the driver's seat as Chase slid into the passenger side.

"Don't worry," Job said as he gunned the engine and the car screeched forward. "We may have one last chance at getting your partner back."

JACK DRUMMOND

EPILOGUE

Reed slowly blinked his eyes open.

Two figures in white garments stood on either side of the table on which he was strapped. The table itself was situated inside of an all white room.

The last thing he could remember was being injected with some kind of tranquilizer as Tucson fought the hordes of men dressed in black military fatigue who were storming the pueblo, the men Tucson had warned him about just moments before their arrival.

But now Reed had no idea where he was.

Presently he thought of Tucson, and of where the old man could be. His eyes had been glowing orange, an aspect that caused Reed to think of the Atoka Research Facility, of the man called Carlton Winthrop, who had been possessed by some kind of insect-like creature.

He had no idea where he was, no possible way of knowing the identities of the men surrounding him.

He was quite literally trapped in the white.

The two men in white garments

appeared to be working with something on his chest, and he tucked his chin into his sternum so as to get a better look at what they were doing.

He saw his chest slit open, his heart thumping, his lungs, ribs, liver, intestines, and all major organs that he could identify at first glance. His heart rate suddenly increased, and he watched as it did so. Suddenly one of the men reached over and forced his head back onto the steel table on which he lay, strapping his head to the surface of the table with a cold metal latch.

Now all he could see was the white.

"What're you doing to me?" he screamed.

No response.

He could feel their presence in the room with him, yet he could do nothing.

"What's happening?" he shouted.

Nothing.

Only his own voice echoing back to him off the walls.

And as he lay there, one thought entered his minD and lingered there. No matter how he tried, he could not force this particular thought out. Like a leech, it had attached itself to his mind, to his very being.

And he could not rid himself of this one thing.

"CHASE!" he screamed, hoping against hope that maybe, just maybe, she would be near enough to hear him.

But he knew she could not.

He knew she was someplace else, someplace so far away. Yet he hoped that by some small means, she would come to his rescue.

She was all he had left.

And as the only therapy he knew for that lingering thought, he opened his mouth, drew another breath, and screamed once more as loudly as he could.

"CHASE!"

Presently, his screams died away, the two men left the room, and all that Malcolm Reed was left with was the white.

TO BE CONTINUED. . .

JACK DRUMMOND

COMING SOON

BOOK THREE

OF

THE COLONIZATION SERIES

BY
JACK DRUMMOND

JACK DRUMMOND

ABOUT THE AUTHOR

JACK DRUMMOND

Jack Drummond grew up in Eastern Kentucky and Southern West Virginia. He currently resides in the hills of East Tennessee and makes frequent trips back to his hometown. He enjoys harnessing his artistic writing skills to craft thrilling scenes and stories in his works of fiction.

Jack published his first book, ICE, when he was fourteen, an accomplishment many considered worthy of much recognition. SHADOWS is the second of a currently unknown number of books in the COLONIZATION SERIES that Jack is currently writing.

His other works include many short stories, several of them encompassing his new, experimental writing style he is calling POINTLESS NOSTALGIA.

Jack has been published several times by the website Rope and Wire.com, a website specializing in western short stories; a genre Jack considers a personal favorite.

A NOTE FROM THE AUTHOR

Well, Book Two of the Colonization Series is finished...I really hope you have enjoyed it.

Book Three is still to come, and I hope you are ready for more twists and turns and weird encounters, because as of this moment, the action and suspense is only just getting started.

Keep up to date with all the notifications and upcoming book signings, as well as keep check on the series by visiting the official JACK DRUMMOND Facebook page. Just be sure to send me a friend request along with a message saying that you are a fan, otherwise I'm not likely to accept you.

Or, if you have any questions or would just like to give me some feedback or just want to chat, shoot me an e-mail at:

jackdrummond15@yahoo.com

Matthew 18:11

May God Bless You,
Jack Drummond

JACK DRUMMOND

SHADOWS

JACK DRUMMOND

LaVergne, TN USA
30 March 2011
222224LV00001B/191/P